Bones of the Apocalypse

Frequency House

Tim Evans

Frequency House, Swansea, SA2 0DN
First Published in the U.K. in 2021 by Frequency House
Copyright © Tim Evans 2021
Editor: Gwion Iqbal Malik, Frequency House
Printed in KDP.

British Library Cataloguing in Publication Data
A cataloguing record for this book is available from the British Library.

Tim Evans has asserted his moral rights to be identified as the author of this work in accordance with the Copyright, Designs and Patents Act 1988.

No part of this publication may be reproduced, stored in a retrieval system, or transmitted in any form or by any means, electronic, mechanical, photocopying, recording or otherwise, without the prior permission of the copyright owner.

Although the author has drawn on his life experience in his work, the poems are works of fiction and no inferences should be made to real people, whether still living or not, unless particularly specified.

Images © Tim Evans and as copyright indications listed.
Illustrations by Tim Evans and Rhoda Thomas.

Other poetry by Tim Evans (illustrated by Anja Stenina)
Do You Want Some (2015), *Exit 42* (2016).

Towards a Poetry of Resistance

It's midnight. It's dry now but it's been torrential, almost tropical rain all day and most of the evening. My cats no longer luxuriate on warm doorsteps but gaze glumly at the tides of water streaming past the window. Like them, I'm safe for now. But outside, in real time, the world continues to unravel. Capitalism provides us above all, we are told, with choice, and right now the choices it offers us are ugly ones. Plague, nuclear war, environmental catastrophe, fascism, or any combination of the above.

Media commentators are more ready to contemplate the end of the world than the end of capitalism. Poets, however, should not be so coy. The system is well past its sell-buy date – indeed, for the vast majority of us it was always inedible and should have gone to the landfill years ago. We are not confronted with Francis Fukuyama's 'end of history' but, rather, an intensification of it, because only in times like this can we make a radical break from the past.

The revolutionary Commune of 1871 was a response by the working class of Paris to war and invasion. The wave of European revolutions and attempted revolutions from 1916-1920, of which the Russian one was the foremost, exploded out of the devastation of World War one and a deadly pandemic that infected a third of the world's population. We are not helpless, but it is only through our own struggles, and, I believe, through social revolution that we become able to create our own future.

Some of these poems relate to the Coronavirus pandemic, but many do not. Some are about racism, the courage of the Palestinians, the Grenfell disaster, deaths in police custody or the treachery of politicians. Some are memories of my road trip across the USA in 1968 or are tributes to the music of the Grateful Dead and Janis Joplin and the poetry of Allen Ginsberg.

Some are celebrations of love in its many forms, ecstatic and otherwise, memories of childhood, or eulogies for friends who left us too soon. Some are about violence, crime and addiction. Some are phantasmagorical journeys through hallucinatory landscapes of death and renewal. Some are about my cats.

They were all written between 2017 and 2021. In effect, they chronicle the years of turmoil, chaos and resistance that immediately preceded the coming of the global plague – and the impact of the plague itself. We now stand on the brink of massive, convulsive changes in which we all - poets, workers, activists, but especially refugees, the stateless, the people of Palestine, people of colour and the huge populations of the global South – will be tested to the limit.

Leon Trotsky, revolutionary, writer and leader of the Russian revolution and the Red Army, said in the 1930's "In our epoch of convulsive reaction, of cultural decline and return to savagery, truly independent creation cannot but be revolutionary by its very nature…" It is in this spirit that I offer you these poems.

In love and solidarity.

31st August 2021

Table of Contents

Towards a Poetry of Resistance

Early Entrances   9

If I Were To Meet You
Daci Goes To Work
Falling Child
Car Park
A Visitation

Summers of Love   20

For Janis
Dancing With The Dead
Incident At Twin Falls, 1968
20th July 1969, Off The Island Of Vis

Plague Years   33

The Wolves Are Out Tonight
The Bastard Is Still Out There
The Plague Year
I Am Not Here
If The Dead Can't Call For Justice
Viral Overload
Spit For The Swallow

Enemies And Friends   52

What's Worse Than A Tory?

Who Killed Grenfell?
Face Of A Soldier
Bones Of The Apocalypse
Freedom Song
Stand Aside
Vigil For The Christchurch Mosques
A Death After Contact With The Police

Jackstown And Pompey   73

Holy Hafod Howl Nightmare
Mozarts Blues
Ode To The Tenby
In Portsmouth there was a man
Early Morning, Highland Road

Early Exits   90

For Vijay
Eddie
a text at 8:21
Nightmares of the Heart
Cat

Dark Matter   101

Crows and Fishes
Black Moonrise
strange crimes
The Keys to the Kingdom
Tales of the Seaside Cities

Last Orders   115

The Holy Fool's Manifesto
The Priests Of The Church of Culture
The Poetry Of Slaves
The Mercy of our Flesh
The Hangman's Cough
Any Last Requests?

Acknowledgements   134
Reviews   142

Early Entrances

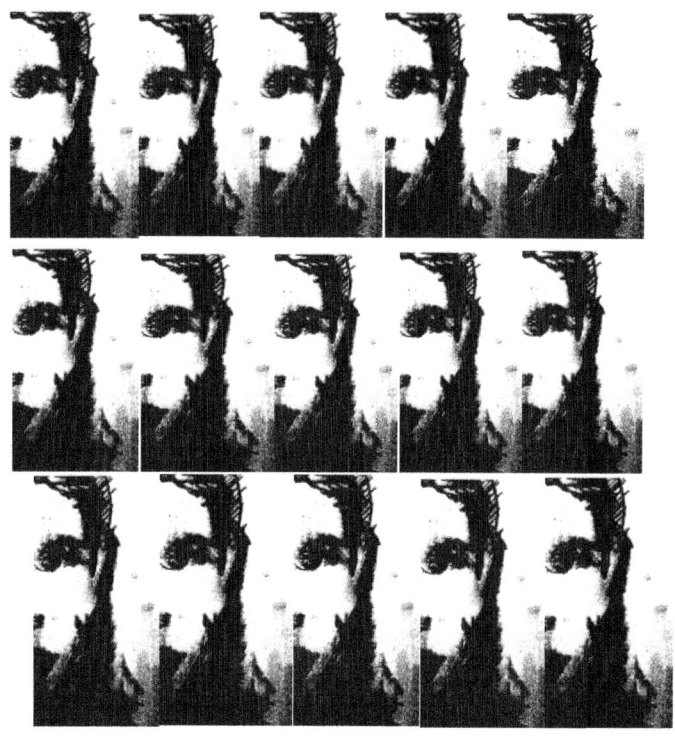

If I Were To Meet You

If I were to meet you
Down by the harbour wall
As the shadows start to lengthen
And the seagulls wheel and call

Where the waves cry to the shoreline
And the sunlight dazzles the sea
And I have no expectations
Of a truth to set me free

And if we started out
Just from that time and space
With disbelief and doubt
Banished from the place

Would you come with me upon the ship
That sails upon this tide
Across futures quite untested
And oceans yet untried

And risk it all on the throw of a dice
Where luck is all laid down
Beneath the cobblestones, the beach
And the rocks of the lost and found

And would you voyage with me
To the valleys of the sun
Be my lover, my companion
Until all the days are done

And the present and the past collide
And the shape the spirits take
Are only promises cast like bread
On the belly of the lake.

Daci Goes To Work[1]

The back lane,
Cinder & ash,
Wound its way
Down
To Havard Rd School.

My Daci's painting & decorating van
Rattled off down the lane,
Swirling clouds
Of grey coal dust
Up into the air,

As he – pipe clamped
Between close shaven jaws,
Dai cap set on grizzled grey hair,
Blue overalls splattered with paint –

And his brother Emrys,
The permanent bachelor,
In pebble-thick specs,
Rolling a matchstick-thin ciggie –

Began their journey
Across town
On their epic mission
To paint, saw & glue together

---

[1] Daci – my childhood pronunciation of "tadcu", the Llanelli word for grandfather.

The world.

And I watched from our back door
As the van disappeared
Down the lane
In the cloud of dust
In the early morning sunlight…

Falling Child

Most of my dreams vanish
With the coming dawn
But one has stayed with me
Down all the years.

I was a child falling
From my bedroom
Into the darkness
Of the house where I was born.

I floated to the ground,
Into the hallway, with its fitted carpets
And monk seat.

And on the wall
The oil painting by Edgar - my grandfather -
Which had hung there all the years
Of my childhood. A snow scene,
A church, bathed in the full moon's light.

Dark steeple rising through the night,
Glowing windows calling to the tired traveller.

And a couple, man and woman,
muffled against the cold
Trudging, side by side, through the snow.

And I imagined they were my grandfather,
And his wife, Edith May, who had died,

But who now was alive, walking
With him into the centre of the painting.

In the darkness at my right hand
Was the room where they slept,
With its round, solid wood doorknob.

Years later, after they died, their bedroom
Was turned into a parlour of sorts
With polished coffee table
And chunky white telephone,
A framed print of Tretchikoff's 'Lost Orchid'
above the fireplace.

It was the best room, the guest room,
And we were discouraged from using it
Until we could be kept out no longer.
But now, in the dream, it was still
Edgar and Edith May's bedroom.
So, out of respect
I did not enter.
But went, instead, up the corridor

Towards the living room
With its rippled glass door,
Feeling the gentle click
Of the ball catch
As it rolled from its socket.

And there it was,
Just as I remembered it:
The television, the dresser

With the willow pattern plates,
The sofa, just big enough for two,
In a recess in the wall, embraced by windows.

And seated there my mother and my father.

But in the paralysis of my dream,
they were not flesh and blood
But hard melted stone. Figures
From Pompeii, caught up in the panic
Of a burning city.

I turned away.
I returned to the moonlit church.
I stepped into the painting's dimension, and up the snowy pavement I walked.

The two figures had vanished into the snow and the night.
But I was sure that if I followed along behind,
All the way down that shining silvery path
I would find them.

Car Park

They both know
they will soon leave
returning to the company of others.

So for these moments alone
they lean drunk into each other's eyes
in the car park under the stars.

The moon shines - a coin cradled in a palm.
The gleaming zip of a black leather jacket.

Her lips are wet.

They lean together
against the side
of the white overnight van.

She tugs down his jeans,
his cock stiffens
in her warm hand.

He takes hold of her
through the faded denim,
rolls her
between his fingers.

And so, for a while
they sway,
with growing urgency

braced against the delivery van
until with a gasp and a broken cry
they come
together –

and for the briefest time
are lost
in the swell of the ocean.

A Visitation

Writing a poem, two in the morning,
And a magical visitation
From a spirit, black as night,
Who purrs like a generator,
And fixes me with her bright green eyes.
Holy being stalking the lap of darkness.
Holy spirit, holy cat, bright little living thing,
Walking nimbly through the walls that separate us,
And bringing me greetings and inspiration
From your other world
At two in the morning.

Summers of Love

For Janis

Golden Gate Park,
Late afternoon,
The long summer of '68.
Already the Haight
Was thick with scag.

The speakers were cranked up
To maximum volume.
The thunder of Big Brother and the Holding Company
Shook the park.

Your voice was twisted with pain,
Syllables stretched and strained.

And as the voodoo of the blues
Took over your body and spirit,
You scraped the ribs of that Cuban guiro
As if you wanted to kill it.

We danced
Under the afternoon sun and the shade of the trees,
Air thick with hashish.

And up on the stage you swirled,
Satin shirt floating,
The white fringes of your leather trousers
Whipping your legs as you stamped the platform.

Jesus, your body seemed so slight.
So naked to the storms
Of fate and fortune.
So open to the capacity
Of a bottle of Jack Daniels
To settle the issue -
All issues –
Once and for all.

But what I remember most
Was your face…
And as the last chords of 'Ball and Chain'
Faded away,
And the crowd burst into crazy applause,
(I was in the churned mud
Up the front
And later convinced myself
We had made prolonged, significant
Eye contact).
You looked almost
Angelically radiant.

You were in *your* place
Among *your* people
And it was almost as if
You could not believe
We loved you so much.

And you smiled and smiled and smiled.
And the stomping and hooting
Went on and on and on.

For minute after minute after minute
As the shadows lengthened
In that late afternoon
In the long hot summer of '68.

Dancing With The Dead

Who played poker with the wolf?
Shot down his uncle to get the gold?
Drove the train on too much cocaine
And answered the answer man?

A medicine for the blues
To carry you through life.
Shake them rolling bones
And lay your money down.

Filmore East in '68.
Garcia borne aloft
On acid guitar waves.
Pigpen's whiskey voice
Driving the Lovelight train.
Bass guitar and drums
Speak to each other
In the voices of spirit animals.
A dialogue of psychic jazz,
That old-time blue light
Mescaline magic.

And in the mosh pit mud at Bickershaw
All the pills and hash long gone
Just the hiss of Newkie Brown ring-pulls.
The Dead have been setting up
For an eternity…
The clouds loom dark and threatening.
Garcia steps up to the mic

The opening chords cascade
From the towering banks of speakers.

And at that moment
Bright blades of sunlight stab through the cloud curtain
That hangs almost to the horizon,
And we are bathed in brilliant light.

A tattered cheer goes up
And the band tumbles into Truckin'
And we dance
Through the wind
And the rain
Carried high
On the wings of song
We dance.

And there were impossible coincidences,
Adventures, tearful reunions
Of old friends and lovers
As the music followed me
Down the years
Until on an August night in 1995
I looked out into the moonlight
From a tower block in Hemel Hempstead.
Jerry Garcia was dead.
And the music was over.

So I did the only thing I could:
I played the music.

I played
Deal
The Wheel
Sugaree
Uncle John's Band
Tennessee Jed
Friend of the Devil

But most of all I played He's Gone

And my mind rolled back
To the morning when I heard John Lennon
was dead
And I'd sat and cried, helpless in the face of it.

This music was the soundtrack
To our lives.

And with the passing of these men and women,
With all their stupidities, their flaws and failings,
Passed the hopes and desires of those times,
And the knowledge was borne in on me ever more strongly
That we had not made the break
That we needed
To wrench history from its deadly path.

We had made music
But we had not made the revolution.

And we live, now, with the consequences of that failure,

As plague rages and war and famine stalk the land,
And climate chaos burns the planet.

And in this pandemic lockdown
I drown in the music of the Dead.
Its cadences, its texture, its intonations
Taking me back to the sunlight of California
Before the wildfires devoured it

And I see it as it was then, driving down Highway One
Between the mountains and the sea,
And in the afternoon the music spiralling upwards
through hallucinatory light
And voices coming together
in high lysergic harmony –

In Golden Gate Park in the long hot summer of '68.

Incident At Twin Falls, 1968

A hot day in Twin Falls.
We drive into town –
Wheels spinning up a thick cloud of dust
As we stop at a convenience store
For 7-Ups and Marlboro.

A year has passed
Since the Summer of Love,
And we're on the road
From New York to San Francisco,

Into the outposts of a divided America
Through the deserts of Ozymandias, King of Kings.

Every city, town and village
Has its colony of rebels.
The tribes stick together
In this hostile territory.

Some crazy acid freaks welcome us into their house
To spend the night rapping and smoking –
Before we wake for the last big drive
Down Highway 84
Into the Golden City.

It is midnight
The room hazy with smoke.
On the turntable,
A Chambers Brothers album is playing

And Maria is coming out of the kitchen
With cups of tea
When BLAM! someone kicks open the door.

Two mean-looking guys with crew cuts
Fill the house with the stink of beer
And the smell of rage.

There is a Stars and Stripes hanging as a drape
Between living room and bedroom.
"I've seen good men die for this flag,"
One of them snarls
As he rips it down.

We are stoned and petrified.
They are angry and drunk.
Local boys on furlough
Back from Vietnam.

They've spent the afternoon
Driving around getting wasted,
Cursing the dirty hippies
With a US flag hanging on the wall.
So by the witching hour
They're ready to kick in our front door
And teach us a lesson.

They glare around the room
And zero in on me.
"I'm gonna cut your hair, motherfucker.
You got a scissors?"
The room shakes its collective head.

"Or a knife?"

And then luck flies in at the window
Like a bluebird,
For one of our group,
A bearded biker,
Is a schoolfriend
Of the second grunt,
And they're talking
About old times.
And the tension
Drains away.

And the two guys relax,
Apologise, and after a while leave.

We sink down onto the bean bags
But there's no time for relief
Because suddenly the front door opens
And the first guy returns
To apologise some more.

We desperately want him to fuck off
But he wants to talk.
And tells us a story
About being up above the jungle in a helicopter
With Viet Cong prisoners.

And they question the first one,
But he's tough, he won't talk,
So they throw him out.
And the second one is tough too,

He won't say a word.
So they throw him out as well.

But prisoner number three cracks
And tells them all they want to know.
And now they don't need any of them,
So they throw them all out.

And the guy's laughing
Till the tears roll down his face,
And the scent of booze rolls off him,
Like the smell of napalm.
And we're laughing too,
And after he's finished laughing
He disappears into the night.
And we lie there,
With the sour, bitter taste
That our laughter at the death of men
Has left, like hot coals, on our tongues.

And early in the morning
Our friends give us breakfast
Of coffee and waffles.
And we drive away
Down Highway 84
To where the sun glints
Upon the Golden Gate,
And a white pelican sails slowly
Above the vast blue swell
Of the Pacific.

20 July 1969, off the island of Vis

before time
off the coast of a country
that no longer exists
we sailed,

she and I,
through oily black night
huddled in the bows of a cargo ship
as it ploughed the Adriatic.

wild seas
crested the prow,
drenched us,
forced us back
down the starboard deck
to the greasy bar
where they served
shot glasses of fiery Slivovitz.

a tall Montenegrin
kissed the back of her wrist,
threw his arm across my shoulder,
and gestured at the TV screen
screwed into the wall,
where, in a grey fuzz of static,
Buzz Aldrin danced on the moon.

Plague Years

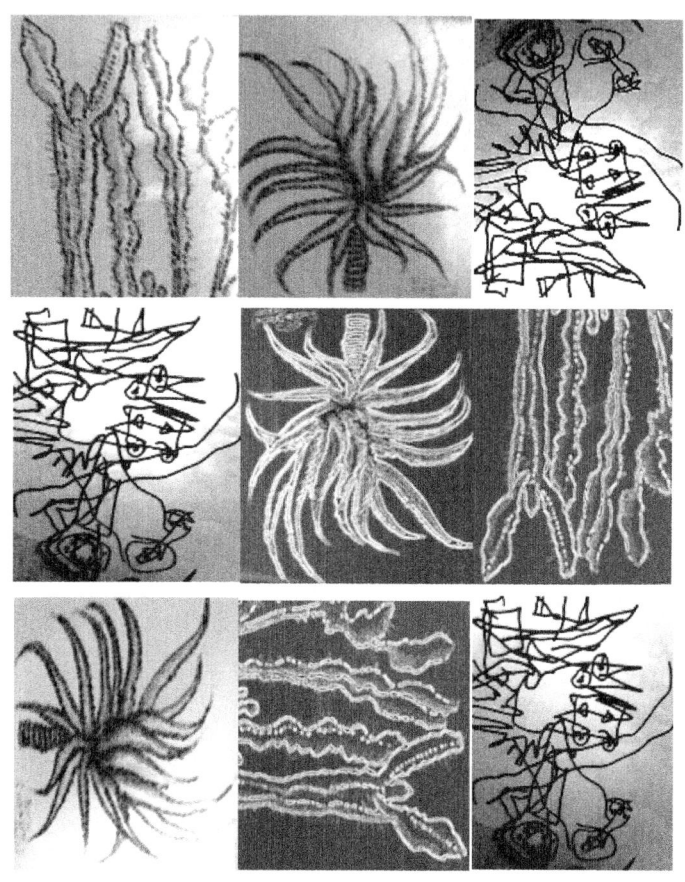

The Wolves Are Out Tonight

The wolves are out tonight
Roaming under starlight
Running wild-toothed in a savage silver stream
Of vicious indifference
Murderers at large
In a dream
That the whole world is dreaming.

It was nothing personal
You have to understand that
Don't get emotional
This is ground zero
There is no tomorrow
And though it's getting late
Nobody's leaving.

Numbers rack up
In this month's streaming
The wolves are coming
Their eyes are gleaming
They stole your breath from your lips
With no apology or warning
It's time to meet death
On this bright summer morning.

The first time as tragedy
The second time as tragedy
Forget the fatalities
We treat them with brutality

We don't have a plan
But we have plenty of mendacity
Let the bodies pile high
We're up to capacity.

They say evil is banal
But combine it with rapacity
Lock it up in a cabal
Whose only centre of gravity
Is a badge on your lapel
It's such a hateful travesty
Such arrogant cowards
Such corruption and depravity.

And we work for the bosses
To kick-start their economy
So that they can compete
With China, France and Germany
While your grandfather
Gets his second tracheotomy
And you are left wondering
Who is really the enemy
When critical thinking
Is thought of as blasphemy.

Government fails
And thousands die in agony
Please for god's sake
Spare us your sanctimony
Which you seem to offer
Without any irony.

Let's face it
You're really not up to the job
You old Etonians
You Charterhouse snobs
You thought this was going
To be a bit of a doddle
Swanking about
In front of the rabble
The hero of Brexit
Nice and simplistic
Arrogant lazy greedy hubristic.

A few years of this
A few years of bliss
Premium grade coke
Nubile researchers to kiss
Feted and adored
And when you get bored
Nice one, Walmart
A seat on the board!

The last thing you expected
You useless sack of piss
Was to be staring
Into a pandemic abyss.

You don't have the qualities
You like a bit of jollity
You wanted the authority
Without responsibility
Without the basic skills
Without the capability.

Like all of your class
You like a bit of flash
You haven't got a clue
What it's like with no cash.

And once we get out
From underneath this tragedy
There'll be scores to be settled
In simple solidarity.

The workers showed the courage
The workers faced death
The so-called unskilled
The exploited and oppressed.

The rich men and oppressors
Showed no backbone no spine
We were led by the worst
At the worst of all times.

And once we get a handle
On the scale of their crimes
It surely can't be far
It surely can't be far
It surely can't be far
To revolution time.

The Bastard Is Still Out There

The bastard is still out there
Out there in the night
The virulent violent virus
Stealing people's lives
With viral downloads, viral fits
Viral overloads, viral hits
Viral truth and viral lies
Viral thieves and viral spies
Viral binbags, viral hats
Viral dogs and viral cats
Viral skulls and viral bones
Viral sticks and viral stones
Viral lager, viral crisps
Viral vodka gets you pissed
Viral spirals viral thighs
Viral flares and kipper ties
Viral hedgehogs viral paint
Viral vinyl looks quite quaint
Viral pissoirs, viral loos
Viral Cuban blue suede shoes
Viral monsters in the dark
Viral neutrons, viral quarks
Viral plagues throughout the nation
Viral angst and alienation
Viral cell contamination
Viral sweat and perspiration
Viral cock-ups, viral blags
Viral glue in plastic bags
Viral mice and viral pigs

Viral guppies, viral squids
Viral coffee, viral tea
Viral speed and ecstasy
Viral dancing in the dark
Viral dreams of Bonaparte
Viral danger in the night
Viral acid satellites
Viral antibody strikes
Viral dips and viral spikes
And the bastard is still out there
Hiding in plain sight
A virulent violent virus
Stealing people's lives
A virulent violent virus
Stealing people's lives
Hiding in plain sight
Hiding in plain sight
Hiding in plain sight
The bastard is still out there.

The Plague Year

white skies and streets of silence
concrete tongues burnt into walls of flame
a solitary cat black as coal stalks over shivered
spines
shattered ribs coated with viral sauce

clots of corona cowslip spurt into these plague years
this wild pathogenic springtime tarred and
feathered with impossibilities
extracellular concrete embedded in the brutality of
architecture
viral envelopes draped across tower blocks and
bridges
and metal likenesses of phagocytes dangling from
our necks as lucky charms

yellow clouds of pandemic mist
drift above this urban wasteland of lies and
emergencies
as we struggle for life in these strange boulevards of
silence
where our rulers are our enemies and
when the time comes for the poison to overflow its
banks
its plague victims too

and out there in the bubbling pits of contagion and
transmission
prisons, refugee camps and detention centres

we face once more the simple lesson
so easy to understand yet so hard to grasp

we are threaded together in a delicate web of dependence
we need each other
and our blindness to this is the most deadly disease
the most fatal virus

and in this night like any other
in this second like any other
in this life like any other
as we fight for survival
and see our friends and lovers
go down
let us swear by the blood on the hands
of the fools that led us here
that there is no going back

the world that rises from this
will be built in the name of the thousands that died
and out of the lies and crimes
will rise new lives, new loves worthy of the name

because after this,
when the silence lifts
there will be thunder.

I Am Not Here[2]

I am not here to entertain you.
If you want entertainment go to a goddam circus.
I am not here to make you laugh,
Or tickle you with the absurdities of life.

I am not here to brighten up your day.
I am not here to distract you
Patronise you, educate you
Seduce you, sedate you or lie to you.

I am an irritant
Just below the surface of your mind.
I am ideological sandpaper
Scrubbing the skin of your consciousness.

I am a sickness, a virus, a pathogen,
Undermining your finely balanced
auto-immune system.

I'm not a poet, you see. I'm a disease,
running through capitalism's bloodstream.

And this is war unto death.

---

[2]

The poem was written in 2018 – two years before Covid raised its ugly head. It describes the poet as a virus infecting capitalism. Strangely prophetic.

If The Dead Can't Call For Justice

I want to bear witness first of all
To the crimes committed by those in power.
The bankers, billionaires and all
The moneyed careerists and political cowards.

Their system bred this awful plague,
And turned a beautiful planet toxic.
As they mixed disease with the making of food
And burrowed though jungles in search of profit.

Puffed up on premium grade cocaine,
Whole fortunes hoovered up their nose,
When the day of reckoning came
All they could do was smirk and pose.

They cheated, swindled, bluffed and lied
Delayed, U-turned, hid their heads in the sand,
They averted their eyes while thousands died
And drug profits flowed into corporate hands.

Had you or I caused, through criminal negligence
Or simple stupidity, so many deaths,
While other governments had dealt with the pestilence
With fewer resources but greater success

We would have been held to account for our sins
Of omission and commission, blood on our hands.
No amount of justification or spin

Would have cleared us of guilt for those we had damned.

To die struggling for breath in an ICU,
The porters and nurses cast into hell,
The teachers, tube workers, no time off in lieu,
The refugees locked in disease-ridden cells.

A diseased system bred this disease.
To stop the disease, you get rid of the system.
It's managed by murderers, con-men and thieves
A whole array of morbid symptoms.

One day they'll be held to account for their crimes
And until that day we'll never forget
If the dead can't get justice in these times
Then it's up to us to collect the debt.

Viral Overload

It's cold up here
Among the stars.
You know those nights
When there's a trail of electricity
You just can't break?
Well there were nights like that,
Up on the east side of the city,
In dreams where I was rearranging my books
Or taking direction from the flight of birds.

I couldn't find my way home
And there were no other possibilities,
Except the ones you might chew over
In random bedrooms
Lies hooked on a doorknob
A pale blue waistcoat hanging on a chair
A cigarette burning in the ashtray…

Last call for alcohol
The night is ready to close down.
Unless you're one of the lucky ones,
The beautiful people invited to the after-party of time
Tickets are only a few years off your life.
Going once. Going twice
Going three times…

Just hand over my heart, father
It's been kidnapped long enough

And I need it back.

And suddenly I'm walking into
A room full of strangers
A love-song from the ghetto
A car-crash of studied carelessness
Three miles out of town.

And I glance at your face again
Over a half empty bottle of wine
As Cohen's 'The Future' plays
For the third time.

I am at the mercy
Of an old prescription
Sealed and delivered
In phased-out downtown bars
Where I can find no trace
Of a human face

And on a good night there's nothing to feel anyway
Except the pain from the scars
Because I'm coming down fast
And there's no time.

And in the dream
I'm driving down the same road as before.
I've left something important behind
And I can't remember what it is.

And I wake up,
Tears frozen on my cheeks.

And I'm standing facing the house
The stone flies through the air
I hear the sound of breaking glass
The window splits three ways
Fragments fall into the room
And into the street.

And in that moment
I disappear completely from her life
Drawing a line in broken glass
That can't be made whole again
That can't be undone
That can't be mended.
I am free.

Free at last
Under the light of a blackout moon
As the track marks of my life
Split wide open again
Along the fractures of time
And bad faith.

It's colder here
Than it was before.
I'm living in a new world
Of existential rehab
Where connections
Were never built to last.

I'm looking for a place of safety,
With no wind chill and no viral overload,
No rising oceans and no firestorms

Before the winds get stronger
And the rivers run dry

Before the fearful morning
Where I'm standing
Bathed in white light
And the music changes
And the cities
Are on fire.

Spit for the Swallow

Night-time prowler skirting the perimeter
Midnight howler growling in the dark
Broken-down chapel and a sinister minister
Slinging sulphate in the alley where the hound dogs bark.

Electric shock jukebox, skip full of syringes
Scattered confusion at the end of the day
Witch-hunted lies, exile and a lynching
Everywhere heavy with the smell of decay.

We gatecrashed Eden and ended up in hell
Working the Steps one day at a time.
When it's harder to buy it's harder to sell
The bigger the fortune, the bigger the crime.

We partied all night but got shattered on the rebound
The volume cranked all the way up to heaven.
It seems a long time ago now, but just turn round
And it's standing at the corner just like it was then.

And there's one road to glory with no tickets to sell
And the horsemen are riding back home in the dark
Too early to hear the clang of the bell,
Too early to hear the song of the lark.

And here's a spit for the swallow, a spit for the crow
A spit for the children you didn't want to know
A spit in the dust to mix up the clay

A spit in your eye at the end of the day.

The house is red and full of radiation
The virus is crawling all around your door
You're gonna need some pills and a spot of medication
And maybe a visit to the liquor store.

And the night-time prowler is consulting his solicitor
The midnight rambler is scared of the dark
The broken-down chapel is a speculative investment
Sold for six million to a Russian oligarch.

These were the things that weren't supposed to happen
These were the beggars that beggared belief
We made an agreement to liquidate the faction
And you swore you wouldn't bring in the police.

Empty threats in the corridors of power
Tremors so faint you didn't feel them at all
We watched the waves gather from the tall black tower
And the ocean was rising like a great grey shawl.

Times like these are the ruptures in history
The rip in the curtain, the crack in the wall
And through the little cracks the ocean comes pounding
Who can say where the water will fall?

Enemies and Friends

What's Worse Than A Tory?[3]

You know what's worse than a Tory?
Than Boris, Gove or Patel?
Or Thatcher & Co., a priori,
And the other vile creatures from Hell?

You know what's worse than a Tory,
Pampered, smug and well-fed?
And Tories are lower than vermin
That's what good old Nye Bevan said.

You know what's worse than a Tory?
In their party of rulers and kings,
Their party of bankers and wankers,
And sponsors of corporate sins.

I'll tell you what's worse than a Tory –
More hateful and rank than this crew
More loathsome, egregious and churlish
More wretched and arrogant too -

And that's the kind of class traitor
You'll find in the PLP,
Who'd prefer to see Tories in power

---

[3] *From 2015-2020 Jeremy Corbyn was leader of the Labour Party and held out hope for some real change. He was however constantly undermined by members of the Parliamentary Labour Party (PLP). This contributed in no small way to Labour's defeat in the 2019 General Election and his subsequent resignation as Leader.*

Than the likes of you and me.

They pretend that they're there for the workers
But they're really there for the cash.
While they're pimping up their careers
They treat their own members like trash.

You know where you are with your enemy
But these are your enemy's spies -
The boss class's own secret agents
Their trade is in falsehood and lies.

So I asked you: what's worse than a Tory?
Well here are a few. Now you know.
Those who stand on the wrong side of history
Into the dustbin of history will go.

Who Killed Grenfell?[4]

Who was it killed the people of Grenfell?
Who put their lives at deadly peril?
Very well, I'll resign, said Paget-Brown
But it wasn't me who put them down.
I didn't give them the runaround.
I didn't want them out of town.
Their deaths aren't down to my account.
No, I didn't kill the people of Grenfell.

Who was it killed the people of Grenfell?
Who put their lives at deadly peril?
Not us, said the leaders of the TMO[5]
It shouldn't be us that have to go.
We listened, we really listened, you know.
We dealt with their complaints like the seasoned pros
We are, and that our salaries show.

---

[4] On 14th June 2017 a catastrophic fire in the Grenfell tower block in West London caused 72 deaths and 70 injuries and made hundreds homeless. At the time of writing, the police investigation into the fire continues. The then Shadow Chancellor, John McDonnell, said that the fire amounted to 'social murder', that political decisions led to it and that those responsible should be held to account.

[5] TMO – Tenant Management Organisation – in this case, it was the Kensington and Chelsea TMO, whose former Chief Executive was strongly criticised in the report into the fire for his "passive role" and "ineffective leadership". Following the fire, Kensington and Chelsea Council took back responsibility for housing in the area. The KCTMO now exists for a single purpose: to be accountable to the public enquiry arising from the fire.

No, we didn't kill the people of Grenfell.

Who was it killed the people of Grenfell?
Who put their lives at deadly peril?
Not me, said Housing Minister Barwell.
I was always a hundred per cent impartial.
My door was always open wide, as normal.
We had endless meetings, minuted and formal.
My interests were in no way commercial.
No, I didn't kill the people of Grenfell.

Who was it killed the people of Grenfell?
Who put their lives at deadly peril?
Not us, said the 72 Tory MPs.
We never voted down that amendment, you see,
To make rented properties safe and clean.
And while we're all landlords, as it seems,
We didn't kill the people of Grenfell.

Who was it killed the people of Grenfell?
Who put their lives at deadly peril?
It wasn't me, said Boris Johnson.
I closed 10 fire stations? That's just nonsense.
The Knightsbridge one was of special importance.
Just next to Grenfell, by all the evidence.
Thank God I don't have that on my conscience.
No, I didn't kill the people of Grenfell.

Who was it killed the people of Grenfell?
Who put their lives at deadly peril?
Not us, said the British government.
You can't threaten any of us with imprisonment.

A bonfire of regulations, that was our sentiment.
Health and safety just filled us with merriment.
For business and profits, there must be no impediment.

No, we didn't kill the people of Grenfell
We didn't kill the people of Grenfell
We didn't kill the people of Grenfell
We didn't kill the people of Grenfell.

Face Of A Soldier[6]

A static image, anchored
In the moment the photo was taken.
Four soldiers, loaded with heavy weaponry,
Body armour, olive-green field dress and steel-capped boots
Dragging a 12 year-old boy
Towards an armoured car.

The boy wears a Spider-Man T-shirt
And blue tracksuit bottoms with an F.C. Barcelona decal.
His flailing feet can't touch the ground,
Because the soldiers have hoisted him in the air.
One of his battered trainers lies in the rubble behind him,
Lost forever in the sand as they carry him
Ever closer to the armoured car.

His face is slick with tears as he begs and pleads.
When the begging doesn't work he kicks and screams.
For his friend Rashid

---

[6] *The creation of the state of Israel in 1948 involved the ethnic cleansing of the Palestinians - an event known as the 'Nakba' or Catastrophe. Each year approximately 500-700 Palestinian children, some as young as 12 years old, are detained and prosecuted in the Israeli military court system. The most common charge is stone-throwing.*

Was snatched only three months ago,
And he never came back.
He pleads that he is only on his way home,
That his little sister is waiting for him,
That he never threw any stones.
Please, mister, let me go.

He is a child. A child of Hebron.

Three of the soldiers are wearing visors
So their faces are not visible.
But the fourth has his helmet pushed back
So that you can see his face clearly,
Frozen in that second.

He is a new recruit, a pale-faced teenager,
Not yet brutalised.
And in that frozen second his unguarded face tells all,
His look is guilty, furtive, frightened,
Even though he is the one clad in body armour,
And toting a Galil assault rifle.

He stares over his shoulder to see,
Not if there are any witnesses,
That does not worry him,
But, with that guilty glance,
He's afraid that God is watching.

It is a haunted glance that knows
That if this is his future,
Then every time he pulls the trigger

He blows a piece of himself away,
Until to do this bloody job
He must condemn all Palestinians
To the same realm
Of the Untermenschen
To which the German Jews
Were sent.

And in that moment
In the horror frozen on his face
He sees, like other oppressors
Who have come before him,
To Ireland, to India, to South Africa,
That he stands at the wrong end of history

And for him and for his masters
This war is already lost.

Bones Of The Apocalypse

Crisis. The mask slips.
Grotesque monsters live.
Bones of the apocalypse
Shaken through a sieve.

Kiss my arse, this is farce,
They think that we're too weak.
Gripped in the lips of the eclipse
So much dead meat.

Capitalism
Always built on blood
Cannibalism
Free market fight club.

No gods. No saviours.
This task is for us.
This gang of thieves won't save us
Nor this assembly of disgust.

Neither Washington nor Brussels
Westminster or Berlin
Nor the kingdom of heaven
Nor the beaches of Devon
Nor the killing fields of sin.

The people have the power
If only we're united.
Praise Marx and pass the powder

And don't let us be divided.

Only the masses have the strength
To turn this world around
And self defence is no offence
On this dark battleground.

Crisis. The mask slips.
Grotesque monsters live.
Bones of the apocalypse
Shaken through a sieve.

Freedom Song

There are those who would divide us
Their reasons are quite plain
Downtown racists strut their stuff
Pumped up on cheap cocaine

Brecht said the beast was still in heat
That spawned the camps of death
The corporate zombies of the elite
Have nothing to express

Except to make us fear and hate
Another's skin or creed
Leave drowning children to their fate
And laugh while others bleed

But we outnumber the dogs of hate
And unity is strong
The fate of my brother is my own fate
And I sing my sister's song

We sing together, side by side
Muslim, Christian, Jew
Black and brown and gay and straight
Trans and lesbian too

For love is stronger far than hate
And love is what we pay
And love is where we seek to be
At the ending of the day

So care for the refugees who flee
The wars our governments sowed
British ministers sipped their gin
As the bombing was proposed

Bogus kingdoms signed and sealed
And delivered to the CIA
Who sent a memo: "Just leave us the names
Of the people to betray."

So stand with those who flee all wars
In solidarity
As we stand with our class across the world
In our longing to be free

Stand with all of the oppressed
No more an internee
Tear down the prisons and the jails
All people shall be free.

Stand Aside

These are not normal times
This is not business as usual
Not a time for nursery rhymes
Protocols or worn-out rituals

The world is hungry for other things
Things that you can never offer
Water from the mountain springs
Wealth within a common coffer

Your jeering future insults our lives
Obscuring memories of the sun
If we wish just to survive
We must undo what you have done

So stand aside, you stink of corruption,
Your time has come, now it has gone
The only politics worth a damn
Protects the poor from the strong

The only politics worth a damn
Is not aimed at the distressed
But stands with the workers and the poor
And fights for the hungry and oppressed

The only politics worth a damn
Will make the walls of the city shake
And turn the old world upside-down
For what power builds, the street unmakes.

Vigil For The Christchurch Mosques[7]

A rainy evening, thick with cloud,
The best part of the day long past,
I stood, part of a silent crowd,
As the ghosts of the dead went drifting past.

We have to reach for the human heart,
The human touch, the human mind
When demons hop and lives are smashed
And love is broken, deaf and blind.

So we stood on the pavement, slick with rain,
And our voices reached out to the stars,
And we reached out to each other's pain
Like an old song played on an old guitar.

But love alone is not enough
On a night so full of human hurt,
And peace won't come if the price of peace
Are bodies broken in the dirt.

'Never again', we used to say.
Well, 'never again' is coming fast.
We stand united – we stand as one,
Against these monsters from the past.

---

[7] *During Friday prayers of the 15th March 2019, a white racist opened fire at two mosques in Christchurch, New Zealand. He killed 51 people and wounded 40. In Swansea, South Wales, a vigil, at which I read this poem, was organised in solidarity with our Muslim brothers and sisters.*

We stand as one – we stand together
In power, hope and unity.
Strike my brother, strike my sister
And you strike me.

A Death After Contact With The Police[8]

Strange how easily people – especially black people – die after contact with the police.

One went into cardiac arrest

Another died from cerebral hypoxia

Another died from postural asphyxia

Another died from self-inflicted asphyxiation

Another had a heart attack at the police station entrance

Another died in a coma four days after being restrained

Another died face down on a hospital bed

Another lost consciousness after being restrained. He could not be resuscitated

---

[8] *Dedicated to all those who died 'after contact with the police' and to their families, friends and comrades who fought, or are still fighting, for justice. Capital punishment was abolished in Britain in 1969, but clearly some didn't get the memo.*

Another was held down for fifteen minutes by four officers. After he stopped breathing they called an ambulance. When it arrived he was dead.

Another was handcuffed and shackled by nine policemen. He was taken to hospital where he also died.

Another was in contact with over fifty officers during the final hours of his life.

The official reports said:
"Police actions did not contribute to the deaths."
"Injuries from restraint were not found to be the cause of death."
"Reasonable and proportionate levels of force were found to have been used."
"There was insufficient evidence to prosecute any officers."

And so, it goes on. These vanishings.
Disappearances. Brothers, fathers, sisters, children.
Magical spontaneous deaths
Slow motion obliterations.
Behind triple-locked and double-bolted doors,
Effects with no apparent cause.

So many questions.
So many lies.
So few answers.
So little justice.
Just one more death after contact with the police.

Jackstown and Pompey

Holy Hafod Howl Nightmare[9]

Om Sri Maitreya
Om Sri Maitreya
Om Sri Maitreya
Om Sri Maitreya

Holy holy holy holy
Holy holy holy holy
Holy holy holy holy
Holy holy holy holy

I witnessed the best brains
Of my tribe crushed by insanity
Ravenous, crazed, helpless

I witnessed the best brains
Of my tribe crushed by insanity
Ravenous, crazed, helpless

I saw, floating in the methamphetamine connections of naked cities,
Deconstructing the cock and balls of bebop
Drinking turpentine and Coca-Cola in Dyfatty Flats
From Gendros to Cwmbwrla and back to Plasmarl
Shuddering, hollow-eyed and wasted to fuck
On the bleak battering of the Number 25 bus
Busted by the Man down in Bon-y-Maen

---

[9] Written in honour of the great American poet Allen Ginsberg, author of 'Howl'.

Between the baked bacteria of banshee dust
and Benzedrine blowback
Baptising its bazooka boombox
As it rocks and rolls its way
Through Manselton and Mynydd-bach
To the hydrogen-blown backstreets
Of
Blaen-y-Maes
Blaen-y-Maes
Blaen-y-Maes

Where skull crazy cathedrals blast my brain to
luminous Blakean visions
Of Evening Post hacks, builders' cracks
Wolf packs, Starvin' Jacks
Smoking Semtex and dynamite
In the toilets of the Adam and Eve
When it *was* the Adam and Eve

In existential subway visions
Breaking down all drear and drained of radiance
On the pukey pavement outside The Potters' Wheel

The Tenby The Tenby The Tenby The Tenby
The Tenby The Tenby The Tenby The Tenby

With ECT, tranquillisers, antidepressants
Up the Coed again staring blankly
At yakkety-yakking hours
Of daytime TV
Jeremy Kyle and Bargain Hunt
So if you weren't

bipolar paranoid disorder
When you were admitted
you sure as shit were
When you were discharged
Discharged like pus from a sucking wound
Into the *ych y fi* bed & breakfasts of Oystermouth Road
Where *mochyn du* mattresses and plastic sheets
Synthesise into hallucinogenic bodily fluids
To blow your mind completely once and forever

And from Portmead to Penlan
From Townhill to Treboeth
From Clydach to Llangyfelach
I ride the screaming seagull neon vibrations
Of cheap thrills, cheap pills, cheap vodka and ketamine

Because I'm with you in Wind Street
Where you must feel very strange
I'm with you in Wind Street
Where the wild Welsh women wail
All microskirts and fishnets
I'm with you in Wind St
Sharing a smoky blunt
In Salubrious Passage
And a K-Y jelly hand job
Round the side
of the Takeaway Pizza Burger

Where I witnessed the best brains
Of my tribe crushed by insanity

Ravenous, crazed, helpless.

Where I witnessed the best brains
Of my tribe crushed by insanity
Ravenous, crazed, helpless.

OM
OM
OM
OM

Mozarts Blues[10]

Sticky floor squacks
Under pale blue neon
Poised somewhere in between
Atmospheric and squalid

Twelve green bottles glint squintily
Speedy light twitches off the mirror
Spinning the mini disco-ball
Gleaming on the ceiling
Piercing the darkness with blue arrows.

On some nights the blue lights
Sent me echoing back to techno nights
And drum 'n' bass clubbing
In the '90s
At Megatripolis
At Whirl-y-gig

And sometimes
Way, way back
To the deep, deep luminous
Joss-stick blue
Of the Freak Out Night at UFO
In 1966.

---

[10] *Mozarts was a bar and live music venue in Swansea's Uplands. The Howl poetry nights took place there.*

At Mozarts the blue, blue faces
Of Allen Ginsberg
Sylvia Plath
Dylan Thomas
Gazed down, ghostly,
Upon us...

To compère, or read, or perform in Howl
You needed magic in your soul
Pure, pure magic.
Or the blues would eat you alive.

Iqbal, wise-cracking it down to the wire
Mic in one hand, lager in the other
Eve, face white as china
Nose and ear-studded
Against satin blackness
Beside that drunken
Standard lamp
That became Howl's icon
Even though the light it shed
Was so dim that once
I pulled a hamstring
Misjudging the distance
Between the mic stand
And the speaker.

Who was before Eve?
Was there *anyone* before Eve?
Yes - Tyler, Jac, Adam
Stacked up backwards
Fading into the shelves of darkness

In the blue fog of Time.

And then the shower of poets
And what a Howling shower it was:
Sarah, Sam, Stephanie, Siobhan, Sharon, Charlotte
Mark, Matt, Mikey B, me
James, John, Joy
Pete, the POTH posse
Natalie, Nia, Alun, Zoe,
Ami, Gemma, Rhoda, Rebecca
Torrents of students
Jetting through like comets
I can see their faces
But not their names
I may have left you out
And if I have I'm sorry.

And when you stepped
Through that door
Into the red and blue light
You crossed a Time threshold
Into a zone where there was no Time at all.
Nothing.
Except a feeling
That anything
Could happen.

It's Thursday night.
Runny-nosed poetry junkies
Gather clucking under the canopy.
Poetry cold turkey time
Searching for those few minutes

In that luminous window of life
When we offer up our words
On a cold blue Thursday night
At Mozarts.

And although we can't take it with us
It is a place that changed us forever.
We went in as one person
We came out as another.

And we carry its spirit
Wherever we go
Wherever we ramble
Wherever we roam
We carry its spirit
All the way home.

Ode To The Tenby

The Tenby
Was always where
Demons and drunks walked
And staggered.

Back in the '60s
We knew we could always get
Served there.

Llanelli boys,
Under 18,
On the run
From Sosban's Tafia
Of Taliban aunts,
We escaped into drunken afternoons
In sunny Swansea publand,
Wading through the smell of stale beer
And No.6 cigarettes.

No-one knew our faces
On these streets.

We had graduated
From drinking Spanish Sauternes
From the bottle
In deserted Llanelli schoolyards
To finding out which Swansea pubs
Would serve us.

The Tenby always would.

The place had a reputation.
We shuffled nervously at the bar
While the barman served up
The Tenby's cheapest hit –
Cider slops from the plastic container
Below the taps that caught the spillover.

It could be bought, I remember,
For sixpence a pint.
It was known as 'scrumpy', for some reason,
Though it bore little resemblance
To the Somerset cider of that name.
But it was cheap, and it got you pissed…
These were its unique selling points.

Spattered up the wall in the public bar
Was a reddish-brown stain
It was said in whispers
That it dated from when a Mayhill hard man
Had taken a dislike, and a broken bottle
To an enemy's face.
The stain of the spurting blood
Could never be fully scrubbed away.

Later, I scored hash there
From Swansea Pete –
Jesus hair and beard
Thin as a tree in winter
White as a vampire
In a Swansea sky.

The man who taught me
How to use a chillum…
Always good for a quid deal of Afghan black.

Swansea Pete
A very legend in his own lunchtime.
The last time I saw him wasn't in Swansea but London
Near Kensington Church Street.
He looked completely wasted.
"Hey man," he said, "Got any scag?"
I couldn't help him
And although I never saw him again
He must have got his act together
Because I heard later he was back in Swansea

And when I moved back
And went looking for him,
I checked out some of the obvious places -
One of them being The Tenby.
The barman told me
He'd died a few months ago.

As a mark of respect, and to remember him
They'd taken his trademark denim jacket
Framed it like an autographed football jersey
And hung it on the pub wall.

The barman pointed it out to me.
It was more eloquent than a football jersey,
And it was autographed, but in its own way.
Distressed denim and rusted badges

Stains and rips, gashes and slits,
A man's life hung there.

Rest in Peace, man.
Sorry we never managed to meet again.
And sorry you had to split so soon.

The Tenby…
Too wicked to live
Too fast to die.
And although it now kids itself
It is a coffeehouse,
It is merely in denial.
Because spectral speed freaks,
Ghostly junkies and dope fiends
Will haunt that place
For all eternity.
That place where demons walked
That place they called…
…The Tenby.

In Portsmouth there was a man

In Portsmouth there was a man.
Dead now, but back then
Alive as you or me.
A sailor, grounded
On dry land for many a year.
Scraggly beard
On dark grey African skin.
Erratic, alcoholic,
With a good heart
But no memory.

Toni was his name.
He carried with him
A pocketful of biros
And a lined school notebook
Where he wrote down all the information in his life.
Shopping lists, to-do lists
And anything else,
Recalled from street chat,
Pub banter,
Names, dates, times,
All the agreements and transactions
Lies, misunderstandings and broken promises of his life.

He was a drinker
Who had, in his long voyage,
Somehow drunk himself sober,
And who now carried with him,

In the absence of his memory,
A chronicle of his life,
A diary of his days,
The words he had heard and read,
The food he had bought,
The people he had met,
The rum he had drunk,
The cigarettes he had smoked,
The women he had loved.

Did he keep the notebooks
Wrapped with elastic bands,
Stacked up in a dark cupboard
In unstable, tottering piles?
Did he recycle them,
Or burn them down to grey ash
In the rusted dustbin
That stood, crazy and battered
Outside the toilet window?

In Portsmouth there was a man
Dead now, dead as a door nail
But back then alive
As you or me.
And he wrote his life down in notebooks.

Early Morning, Highland Road

From the moment the blues
Came knocking on my front door
I knew the old games were history…

Drifting through Southsea streets
In the last nights of the last century,
One dented djembe, badly in need of re-tuning,
several previous owners…

I spent midnight staring through the cold windows
Down on the chill black waters of the Solent
As the car ferries, big as towns, sailed by…
Moons floated behind ripped rags of cloud,
Footsteps echoed on the stairs, and far
Inside the block I remember music playing, winding
deep into the night with infinite sadness…

Darting from an alley behind the pub
A dog fox, shadowy and sinuous, crossed the street,
Slinking silvery through moonlight.

And I lay on the mattress, somewhere in no-man's land,
Between the fading ghosts of euphoria and a dead reality,
Until at half past five Sally, the Angel of the Dawn,
arrived with my medicine.
I knew she wouldn't stay, even though Miles Davies
was playing.

She shone with slowly fading electrical energy
Like one who hasn't slept for days,
Flying on hardcore chemical powder.
But her voice was like honey…
And she said yes to a coffee and she laughed at my jokes
And I wanted her to stay forever.
Her eyes were naked as night, and when we kissed goodbye her lips tasted
Of black tobacco and sweet Spanish wine.
"I like failure," she said. "It makes you strong."

After she left I walked down to the beach as the day was slowly, greyly dawning
And the light on the sea mist was fading along the strand
And I crunched along the pebbles as far as the Hoverport
And the deserted fairground

Then I came back home and slept
And as I slept I dreamed a dream

And in my dream
I imagined the sea and sky
Yielding to the sudden boom and flash of nuclear light,
And a great mushroom cloud billowing black
As the huge crack of doom
Split open the firmament.

And then I knew.

Early Exits

For Vijay

We forgot how final was the line
Crossed between worlds,
And how in between
One second and the next
You passed into that foreign land,
Return ticket lost forever,
Passport out of date,
Visa invalid,
No identification,
No documents,
No right of readmission.
And still we forgot
How fragile life was,
How unbearably fragile,
And you now out of reach
Of text or Messenger,
Twitter or Facebook,
No words left on your answerphone,
Your mobile mute forever now,
Number not available,
Password invalid,
Username not recognised.
And we are left behind
On alien shores,
Under an alien sky,
Remembering with a shock
How strong the current was.
Remembering with a shock
How we somehow failed to hold on to you.

Remembering with a shock
How grief proves the divinity
Of the human heart.
Remembering with a shock
How much we loved you.

Eddie

"Hi Eddie!" I shouted back.
You'd called down
From the window of the flat next door.
I was filling the bird feeder tubes.
"Them're the fattest pigeons in Sketty Park," you said.
"Can you keep mine filled up?
I'm off to visit the folks tomorrow."
"Off to Donegal?" I asked, "How long are you away?"
"Just a few weeks."
"Yeah sure. I'll keep them topped up".
"Cheers. I'll give you the money."
"Bugger off!"
You smiled broadly
And gave me the thumbs-up.

The flat was quiet while you were away.
Not that it was noisy while you were there.
But I missed hearing the door opening and closing
As you came and went
And the sound of you chatting with your old lady
On the steps
Or suddenly meeting you in the corridor
If we both went out at the same time.

I went away for a while myself
But before I went I filled our bird-feeders
To the brim with the best black seeds.

The nuthatches and the finches
Always liked them best.

When I came back a few weeks later
My flat was cold.
I turned on the heating
And made some tea.

Later there was a knock on the door.
It was the guy from two floors up.
He told me you were dead.
"Brain cancer," he said.
"It went right through him
In a month."

So long, Eddie.
Wherever you are, for me
You'll always be at that window, smiling,
Giving me the thumbs-up sign.
And, yes, I'll make sure
The birds are fed.

a text at 8.21

for mark montinaro

a text at 8.21
man down
a tear in reality

my god. how?

i don't know
i just know he died

christ. i thought you'd live forever
forever. i thought you'd live forever
i wear your absence
like a cloak

he could cast spells, you know
and work magic

fuck this
that ends
so abruptly
with so little time

but sometimes
i swim into our conversation
like a fish
i stay with you
for a little while

then resurface
because you never really died…
you work magic, and in another world
we still talk
like we used to
and I still hear your stories

a text at 8.21
man down
a tear in reality
a tear, a tear in reality

Nightmares of the Heart

I couldn't believe the news that night
In the shining cinema lights
That you had left the world behind
And suddenly took flight.

I said, "There must be some mistake
Some failure to communicate
Some dream from which I must awake
Hidden in this night".

I couldn't believe the news that night
In the fading of the light.
A nightmare hidden in plain sight
Seven curses spoken loud.

A sacrifice for all to see,
Sunk to the bottom of the sea,
I dare you all to disagree
Under the thundercloud.

There is no ragged hunger
For the ringing of the bells
As we cross that fatal threshold
Of our own private hells,

And where our feet are walking
Not a soul on earth can tell
Fall off that broken bridge
To the world beyond the clouds.

Reach a place inside your mind
Where you can never think aloud
Reach a place inside your heart
Where your pride is all burnt out.

Reach a place inside your body
Where no dancing is allowed
Lay down that voodoo, brother
There's no exit out of hell.

I couldn't believe the news that night
As I checked in at the desk
Didn't believe the stars could shine so bright
On the worst and on the best.

I didn't believe the news that night
When nothing is as it seems
Goodbye, goodbye, lay your burden down
In the valleys of your dreams.

Lay your burden down, lay your burden down
Heal your bitter wounds and scars
And strew your glory and your love
Among the scattered stars.

Cat

Sad, sad morning
My cat is dead

Such a beautiful
And loving cat

Slight, slender
With a light touch on life

He would lie in my lap
And sleep long and deep

We would rub
Our heads together

His purring
Was a constant low vibration

And sometimes
He would look straight at me

With his piercing
Green eyes

As if he knew
Everything about me

I named him Noah
After Noah Ablett the rebel miner

And sometimes he was exactly that
Anarchist wildcat

The black agitator
Of wildcat strikes and sabotage

He had no fear
And he loved well and deeply

It was fearlessness
That led him out into the road where he died

And now his broken body lies silently
In my room

And I blow smoke upon him
And make my Kaddish prayer for his great soul

Goodbye my Noah
My most wonderful cat
You lived briefly but beautifully
With great grace and loveliness

And I am proud and privileged
To have been your friend.

Dark Matter

Crows and Fishes

The stars stare down like silver
On the angels in the snow
And on the angels' killer
And on the carrion crow.

The old year turns its crooked back
Its bones poke through the skin.
I follow the eternal tracks
Of the twisted shape I'm in.

It was never my intention
To steal away your face,
For in the fourth dimension
There is no time or space.

The hunting dogs so gaunt and still
That dreamed the moon away
Now course the started hare until
The night bleeds into day.

You knew it would be hours
From the darkness of retreat
Till your life returned to power
In the power of the street.

In the back seat of the car
You pack away the time
And the livid, frost-white scar
Is evidence of the crime.

They thought they could accuse you.
What kind of shit is that?
Slander and abuse you
And take all the money back.

Darkness turns to darkness
As we burn the time away.
The dead year's withered carcass
Is the final giveaway.

The crossroads and the threshold
In transition must be marked.
So tightly tie the blindfold
Around your bleeding heart.

Sliding through the seaside city
In the slippery coils of Time.
The Campaign Finance Sub-Committee
Isn't worth a dime.

Time runs at a different speed
At the dying of the year
But what you think we both agreed
Was what you wished to hear.

The old year tilts to tipping-point
The world slides off its back.
It dies from cancer, Aids, TB,
Stroke and heart attack.

Yes, time runs at a different speed
Tomorrow and today,

Running down the endless streets
Of an empty cabaret.

Landscapes of myth, landscapes of mind
Of dreamworlds past decay.
The wounded are healed, and the stone-cold blind
Will recover their sight today.

Strange times are coming, facing off infinity
Emergency a state of mind,
Fearful antithesis, fearful symmetry,
Sealed, delivered and signed.

And there was nothing I could do
No mountain I could climb.
Some of it was false and some of it true
But most of it was out of time.

And the rock'n'roll women kicked off their shoes
And let down their oiled-up hair.
You can find them wherever they sing the blues
To keep away despair.

And the tears ran down a burning face
And onto a handkerchief.
They stood in the sun under God's disgrace
No fear, no sorrow, no grief.

It was the wrong bouquet and the wrong time of day
And the wrong end of the month.
No need to go down on your knees and pray

Because you can't die more than once.

The seventh sun fell from heaven.
You could hear the jackdaw's cry.
The Dice Man called out seven-eleven
And the starlings wheeled in the sky

And the winter's silence lay on the earth
And there was no need to reply
And life was death and death was birth
And the stars fell out of the sky.

Black Moonrise

Black moonrise in an iron darkness.
A cold wind comes
Dragging sacks of dreams
Over a wounded landscape.

Creeping through the cracks in my bones,
Using the shattered fragments
To build ragged towers
All the way to the stars
And back again.

A cold wind blows from the north.
Winter is coming.
Winter is coming.

Under the hawthorn tree
The twisted body of an angel
Lies half-buried in the snow.

Sometimes it feels like all I've ever known
Is winter.

Something waits.
Obscuring memories of the sun,
Leering in its face
Until all that is left is the darkness
And the glittering of rough poetry.

Dogs that were grey at the kill

Slouch by my side as the hunters return
Black against the moon
Trotting through winds of ice.

A cold wind blows from the north.
Winter is coming.
Winter is coming.

strange crimes

strange witnesses
to strange crimes
strange sicknesses
and strange signs
strange silence
when the music dies
strange promises
and strange lies

a strange stranger
on a pale horse
asks me now
as a matter of course
is it by design
or is it by force?
is it by blood
or deep remorse?

is it by stardust
hunger or dust?
is it by ashes
or is it by lust?
is it by fire
or is it by ice?
or is it just another
throw of the dice?

is it that last debt
you still have to pay

when the money's due
at the end of the day
and the last door closes
for the very last time
on your promises, your lies,
and your precious crimes?

The Keys to the Kingdom

It's only the ghost train in winter
It's only a cloud in the sky
It's only the blues coming at you
It's only the mote in your eye
It's only a golden medallion
Of horse blood and neatly cut hate
It's only those men coming for you
Let's make America great

And when the estates of the holy
Are wrapped up in ribbons and blood
And you deal with the death of you only
Shot down in the Arkansas mud
And no preference is best in this matter
In this drunk tank of vodka and gin
You could leave the whole world here in tatters
Because the night time's the right time for skin

So what moral is there to this story?
What moral is there to this song?
There's a staircase that leads you to glory
There's another where you don't belong
And while everyone runs for the money
We all try to act like we're saints
And I tell you my friends it's not funny
When you're hit with some heavy restraint

So my brother he came for the money
And my father he came for it too

And there's something that told me my honey
That it was too good to be true
So say, is your hate hard to swallow
When you're lost in the Mexican rain?
Should I bust you or should I just follow
That parcel of thieves in your brain?

The blood makes pools on the pavement
From the wounds in the body of Christ
The speed-freaks are down in the basement
Freebasing on uppers and ice
You were crucified for incitement
A thousand miles back in the day
But the bastards never would tell you
Who they needed you to betray

And it's one for the one-eyed Jehovah
And it's two for the blood of the lamb
It's three for the scales of the serpent
It's four for the horns of the ram
It's five for the keys to the kingdom
It's six for the beast from the sea
It's seven-eleven for the daughters of heaven
And it's eight for the nails in the tree

Tales of the Seaside Cities

We spiral from the grimy sky
Broken like a leaf
And neither birth nor death-in-life
Will bring us sweet relief
For nothing counts for nothing
In the litanies of grief.

Ambiguous fishbone evenings
In the pouring rain
While we do nothing more than smile
At our ugly, twisted pain
Down empty galleries of dust
While fat worms eat our brains.

One day of greed upon your cheek
In the blindness of your breast
Breathless in the darkness
As I lie down and confess
And lay my urgent hands upon
Your utter nakedness.

Holding those hidden moments
Where I only see your face
And chase your after-images
From place to holy place
Where the secrets of your body
Can never be defaced.

You hold euphoria's promises

Tattooed inside your thigh
Ripe within the warm
And dappled chambers of the sky
And the slow sweet itch of hunger
Grows behind your lidded eyes.

Until one morning I awake
And all I had is gone
There is no consolation
In the hollow, wasted dawn
And all I give and all I take
Is void of shape or form.

No matter the prescription
We are always on the edge
Spinning dreams of vertigo
As we inch along the ledge
Of the cliff tops crowned with nightmares
And the spare change of the dead.

Roadkill can't redeem us
Scavenged by the crow
Cast to the dogs of fortune
Who know all there is to know
As seconds pass, some slow, some fast
And hours still to go.

There are no answers I can give
Here in the pouring rain
There are no bets that I can lay
To take away your pain
No final proof, no holy truth

No lies I can't explain.

And when at last it all comes down
Stark naked and absurd
We lose our pointless knowledge
To the singing of the birds
And folly turns to wisdom
And wisdom turns to words.

For nothing counts for nothing
In the valleys of belief
And neither birth nor death-in-life
Will bring you sweet relief
And spiralling from the grimy sky
Drifts the broken, frozen leaf.

Last Orders

The Holy Fool's Manifesto

And ding dong I was jettisoned
Into a world I never knew
With not a drop of medicine
For when the fuses blew

Which they did pretty regular
More than people knew
So I'll put my money on the bar
And I'll tell you a tale that's true

There was something wrong with the wires
They were connected together all wrong
Because to sing in the heavenly choir
First you've got to think of a song

And when your mind's so totally empty
It's a shame to confuse it with thoughts
Candy for the cognoscenti
Who bought what should never be bought

I didn't want to be a mad genius
I didn't want to be a saint
Some days I was tired and squeamish
I couldn't participate

Some days it was all that I could do
To drag myself through the day
Outstanding payments were always due
Who was I to disobey?

I needed something to speed me up
And something to calm me down
In a system that was irredeemably corrupt
Full of chancers, fools and clowns

There were no redeeming features
But there were shadows on the wall
And I was the son of a preacher man
And I couldn't afford to fall

In a world of constant rephrasing
Of words that made no sense
Of addictions, lies and cravings
Of anxiety and suspense

Where broken pieces of silence
Float where no sounds exist
And the certainty of surveillance
Hangs like an iron fist

I pieced together the mosaics
Again and again and again
A quail's egg pickled in aspic
And smeared on the windowpane

Does it make sense now? Did it ever?
Yes? No? Maybe not?
You'll remember this forever
Till your lights and liver rot

It was dead before I said it
The lies were scrawled in sand

The nightmares were made for misfits
And the dreams were second hand

The pictures were put together
From the splinters in my head
And the dealers took their pleasure
From the souls of the living dead

And the final realisation
Came with blinding light
There's no final negotiation
With a phantom that you can't fight

Would you deny the weather?
So weather your disbelief
You can crawl through life forever
Impaled upon your grief

It came wrapped up in that Brando line
That knocked you on your ass
"I coulda been a contender, Charley
I coulda had class"

Born into a world I never knew
And could not understand
There was no time paid off in lieu
Under my father's hand

A kaleidoscopic journey
From that San Vittore cell
To the office of the District Attorney
And various lesser hells

Jiving in the forest at midnight
In microdot confusion
Those visions of acid insight
Were just another illusion

And stalking the heart of darkness
Was no job for a saint
The wildfires in the cosmos
Drew no noticeable complaints

I've spent a million lifetimes
In a million different shapes
With no compass, maps or lifelines
Just the tyrannies of fate

So when the last piece of the last jigsaw
Finally fell in place
There was no mystical enigma
Just the image of my own face

But like a Holy Fool I made it
Through the flames and the showers of shit
Although the sunflowers had all faded
And the jury wouldn't acquit

There's nowhere else -
The plague's abroad, Godot's lost at sea
There's a hundred million people
Which of them is me?

The world falls apart, but the pieces fall
In a million different ways

We knew we were in for the long haul
When we entered the second phase

And the second fiddle became the first
And we lost all rhythm and rhyme
And the best among us became the worst
And the angels flew backwards through time

And we threw off grief, it was all used up
This is me, and this is you
And this is now: the only place that's left
To deal with what is true

We reach understanding as the mountains split
And the stars come falling from the sky
And the lightning hisses and the thunder hits
And the tide is swelling high

And some deadly god is fashioning a tune
From the bone inside your thigh
No time for omens, for prophecies and signs
No time to ask them why

This is no time to get wasted
You're going to need a clear head tonight
Your contract's terminated
And it's time to rejoin the fight

The details of the day have vanished
In the ocean of your mind
And your crimes have gone up the tariff
Sealed, delivered and signed

And a thousand riders breast the hill
Tattooed on the skin of the sky
Promises yet to be fulfilled
Are a kind of battle-cry

The world we knew is vanishing fast
Have the courage to seize the day
It's from broken worlds that fall apart
That new ones can be made

People rise up, for we are the force
To lead us from this hell
Trace the river back to its source
Draw the water from the well

Fight the power, or it will kill you
There is no middle way
All that they will tell you
Is which people to betray

The Holy Fool's Manifesto
Spray-painted on the walls
Will serve as a memento
For the night this empire falls

For the night the king is killed
And his courtiers swept aside
For the night the old world dies at last
Assisted suicide

And the midnight dancers are playing for time
I can hear the seagulls cry

You can choose your prophecies, choose your signs
And choose the day you die.

The Priests Of The Church Of Culture

We are the Priests of the Church of Culture
And we are here to instruct you
In the arcane paths of creativity
For we are the Priests of the Church of Culture.

We are the Priests of the Church of Culture
We can change mere water to the finest wine
    for we hold the Keys to the Kingdom
Of publishing houses and Arts Council grants
For we are the Priests of the Church of Culture.

We are the Priests of the Church of Culture
We will tell you which words to use
And how to fashion a good commodity
For we are the Priests of the Church of Culture.

We are the Priests of the Church of Culture
We will teach you how to tap your subconscious
How to fill in applications for the National Lottery
For we are the priests of the Church of Culture.

We are the priests of the Church of Culture
You can work your recovery from bad poetry
    and risky Thesaurus dependency
Through our dynamic Twelve Step
    Poetry Rehabilitation Programme
For we are the priests of the Church of Culture

We are the priests of the Church of Culture

And for £965 per person
> we can unclutter your creativity.
It will be an immersive experience
For we are the priests of the Church of Culture.

But there are no Priests
And there is no Church
There is only you, your words, other people
And that is all.

You write because it drives you mad.
You write because it keeps you sane.
For you are the Priest of the Church of Culture
Yes you are the Priest of the Church of Culture.

The Poetry of Slaves

There are no expectations
To reconnect my mind
From the terror of the present
To the tyranny of time

Can I learn the words to speak
Directly from the heart
When I'm trapped inside another's pride
And the soldiers disembark?

Cloaked in splendid emptiness
At the ending of the day
Drawing down the curtains
On the patterns of decay

The power of the ignorant
Destroys the Virgin Birth
And the red blood of the innocent
Scalds the burning earth

I could have trod on broken glass
For the items that I need
For no-one lives by bread alone
When treaties are agreed

And babies' bodies are not news
When they wash up on the beach
But I don't care – compassion
Is more honoured in the breach

Gargantua and Pantagruel
Grow fat on meat and wine
While their weapons kill the children
In the fields of Palestine

And at the gambling table
They are no fathers here or sons
Resistance here was duty
Long before the war began

The broken poetry of slaves
Is etched upon the sky
It's too early now for living
And far too late to die

In the crazy broken sunlight
Where you hide your broken heart
You must decide which genocide
Carries the Devil's mark

For on this wounded planet
Circling a dying sun
The blood and the bread's already dead
And all the mouths are dumb

And in the gaze of your dying face
Tyrannised by fools
Embrace that place in empty space
Where there are no rhymes or rules

But only expectations
On the killing fields of time

For God's own grace won't leave a trace
Of the world you left behind

For the clocks have stopped in the Commune
I can hear the seagulls cry
Minos is nailed to the Holy Grail
And the sun is in the sky

The Mercy of our Flesh

Wounded in the tongue,
Palms braced against a blue moon rising,
Hauling off your scuffed and grimy jeans.

Spreading feverish desperation over belly and breasts,
And slick strands of white peroxide hair
Falling loose upon your face.

Hazy mouthfuls of smoke drift,
And in the midnight hour ululations come easy from cloudy lips,
Softly weeping angels of desire.

Silver skin,
Blind and slippery,
Reflecting smooth puddles on an empty street

As we slide into the warm miracle
Where everything, even death, is as nothing,
And the mortally injured world is bright, immaculate, whole.

Our mouths surrender
And in the velvet darkness
I eat your heart.

And I swear
That I will carry adoration to heaven

Like a swallow piercing the open skies.

And my tongue, sweet in the half-light of dawn
Will serve as an instrument of love
As we discover, at the very last, the mercy of our flesh.

The Hangman's Cough

The gates of Hell swing open wide
And not a bloodstain seen
So much is broken up inside
Like pieces of a dream

And though I yearn to put it off
Until another day
I hear again the hangman's cough
I dare not disobey

The cat goes pacing down the hall
Her shadow follows too
We who are nothing shall be all
And what is false is true

We try, we fail, we fail to try
We lay down on the floor
For God has bigger fish to fry
Behind the kitchen door

Indecision is the curse
The curse that bruised your heart
For there was fire at your birth
That tore your soul apart

And as misfortune builds upon
Misfortune once again
You wonder where your luck has gone

And where they hid your brain

Self-medication is the way
To pacify your mind
Waiting for the man to show
You prophecies and signs

When emptiness is all you know
The sinner is the saint
He brings the charlie and the snow
No need for self-restraint

But burn-out follows burn-out
And your good luck turns to shizz
You can't even dodge the fallout
From your last hit of whizz

The Cowboy said addiction
Will simplify your life
On a heroin prescription
You don't need to think twice

Forget all those ambitions
And dreams from long ago
There's just one big decision
And that's the one you know

And though you yearn to put it off
Until another day
Softly you hear the hangman's cough
You cannot disobey

Any Last Requests?

Playing chess with Death
On a wet and windy shore
Any last requests?
Or shall I go down for more?

Shall I get in some more?
Are there any last requests?
Any kisses in the dark?
Ah, don't look so depressed.

I spend most of my time
To keep you from despair
Wisdom is such a crime
When it's folly undeclared.

Wisdom is such a crime.
I've been down since I could crawl.
Call it soda, lemon or lime,
We're in for the long haul.

Call it soda, lemon or lime
You're left without a prayer.
You knew you'd run out of time
When you saw her standing there.

You knew you were out of time
With no covenants to swear
No portents, visions, signs
No bargains of despair.

You'll be left on the windy beach
At the end of your grand affair
And all will be out of reach
Except dreams beyond repair.

Acknowledgements

Always a difficult one, this. There are so many people tied into the experiences crystallized here that I could easily fill another booklet just with their names. Poets, activists, partners in crime, djembe players, mosh pit maniacs, people who got me out of a tight spot, people who got me into a tight spot, the list is endless. If I've left you out, I apologise in advance. Please feel free to include your name at the bottom of the page, either in your imagination or in biro...

First off is my life partner, fellow-poet, comrade, and co-founder of Live Poets Society, Rhoda Thomas. Her organisational and therapeutic skills have kept me sane during the ongoing madness which is Live Poets, both in our Zoom and social media forays and in pre-pandemic real life. Her love, creativity and encouragement have been absolutely central to the creation of this book.

I also want to send good vibes to Iestyn, my son, and Tesni, Rhoda's daughter. We love them very much, and they keep us sane and grounded.

Next up is my publisher Iqbal Malik, who kick-started Frequency House into existence. Swansea is crying out for a consolidation of its strands of experimental, radical and progressive poetry, of which Live Poets is one. The power of political poetry to bear witness is one of its primary strengths, and in channelling the radical energy in the air, Frequency House can move things onto a new level.

The ecosystem within which much of the poetry in these pages flourished was of course the bar-and-coffee-house-based poetry scene in Swansea, some of it underground, some on the surface. The entrance into this came for me through the Junkbox poetry workshops which met first at the Dylan Thomas Centre and then at Mozarts, a bar and live music venue. It was a dark, beer-smelling sticky-floor kind of a dive, with great vibe and character, where you could always get a late drink when everywhere else was shut. Also at Mozarts was Howl poetry night, which, after Live Poets, in my opinion, is the best poetry night in Swansea. Over the course of a few years Howl had a string of comperes: Tyler, Jac, Adam, Eve and Iqbal. Then, a few years ago, much to our dismay, Mozarts closed. Mozarts Blues is my tribute to the place, a great Swansea venue that I fear we may not see the likes of again.

A powerful influence on me for some years were the fabulous Poets On The Hill, the raucous and chaotic poetry group which emerged after the BBC screened 'Ugly Lovely Swansea: A Poet on the Estate'. In this, members of the community of Townhill staged a production of 'Under Milk Wood', directed by the legendary Benjamin Zephaniah. Several of the original participants, notably Julia Manser, the artist Gemma Elizabeth Collins, Zoe Murphy and Ami

Phillips decided to keep the ball rolling and so Poets on the Hill (POTH) came into being. Living in neighbouring North Hill, and already on the poetry circuit, I ended up drawn into their orbit. When out on the lash on a poetry night, POTH were a force of nature. I shall always entertain fond memories of the poetry and vodka-fuelled chaos that ensued one night when they crashed Howl mob-handed.

Other poetry nights included Talisman at Tino's coffee lounge and later at the Copper Bar, where regular performers included Rebecca Lowe, Mark Lyndon, Tony Webb, David Churchill, Ray Lawrence, Mikey B, Rosy Wood-Bevan, Teifion Hughes and Pete Henson. Another open mic night was Mad As Birds poetry at The Squirrel Café, hosted by the talented Natalie Ann Holborow.

And then of course for the last four years Live Poets Society has tried, as society lurches further into crisis, to channel some of the political energy which is growing – whether around anti-racist struggles, strikes, the Palestinian resistance against Israeli war crimes, the mass movement against climate chaos, the fight against deportations and in support of refugees, the Corbynista days of hope, and the huge Black Lives Matter protests.

Our first performances were at the radical Britpop Café before it closed (what is this thing with poetry nights and venues closing?). Then we moved to Cinema and Co, run by the brilliant Anna Redfern and her team, where we had some amazing years. We were not expecting the nights to take off as they did – one evening we had almost a hundred people in the audience, which for a local poetry night, in a not especially large town, on a Monday night at that, is going some.

I am convinced the huge popularity of the nights (apart from the fact that the performers were bloody good) was because we put on poetry that took sides, that was avowedly political, in the best traditions of the campaigning, radical and revolutionary left. That was what drew so many young people to us. They had given up trying to make sense of things through the narrow prism of official politics, and they knew that the mainstream media outlets lied to them as a matter of course. They had often come to poetry, reading it, writing it and performing it, to make sense of a world that was getting more repressive the more it went off the rails. They were stuck on a planet stricken by massive and destructive climate change that governments didn't want to do anything about, where sexism, racism and bigotry were rampant, and where fascism was once more rearing its ugly head. Live Poets were anti-racist, anti-sexist, we supported LGBTQIA+ rights, we welcomed Muslims, Jews, migrants and refugees, trans poets came and read their poetry loud and proud. Those nights were a safe space where all of us could come together to exchange our experiences and describe our realities through the media of poetry and song.

Videos and stills of demonstrations and protests served as a backdrop as poets read, singers sang and guitarists played. Trade union banners and Freedom for Palestine placards decorated the walls. I particularly want to thank Swansea Stand Up To Racism, whose banner graced our walls for several of the nights in question. Special thanks to Nimi Trivedi and Martin Chapman, and to Alan Thomson, whose IT skills were so important to the smooth functioning both of the nights themselves and to our social media presence, especially after the onset of Covid and our shift online. Also to be acknowledged is Alun Rhys Chivers, who provided Welsh translation for our publicity.

Some outstanding poets performed there with us over the years, including Glyn ap Ifor, National Poet of Wales; the wonderful radical Welsh poet Patrick Jones; Manjit Sahota of Poets Against Racism; the amazing rap and spoken word performer and poet Rufus Mufasa; poet Tessa Foley from Portsmouth; and musicians Neil Clarke and Kate Ronconi, Tom Emlyn of Bandicoot, Tony Webb, Huw and Heather Pudner of the Pontardawe Folk Club and Eleri Angharad during the 2018 release of her album Earthbound. Our initial core of local poets included Phil Knight of Neath, Heather Booker (whose barnstorming poem The Only Red In The Village always brought the house down), Gemma June Howell, Iqbal Malik and Matt as well as Rhoda and myself. Since then, we have been joined by many others including Erika Tregonig, Sierra Moulinié,

Rae and Huriyah Sisuvie. We had some amazing nights there.

Live Poets also participated in the annual commemorations of the 1911 Llanelli Railway Strike and Uprising, including a memorable night at the Carwyn James pub in which Matt displayed a total commitment to his poetry, and audience participation reached new heights. Thanks too to the Rail, Maritime and Transport Union (RMT) for their much-valued support of the Llanelli events.

Although in the pre-plague era our poetry nights were mainly based in Swansea, we did venture further afield. I must pay tribute therefore to Mike Jenkins' Red Poets in Merthyr, Robert Minhinnick's Green Room in Porthcawl, Aida Birch's Cheval in Neath, Dominic Williams' Write4Word Poems and Pints in Carmarthen, Eleanor Shaw's Saturday Spoken Word in Llanelli and to the many fine poets from Blackwood, Cardiff and elsewhere. Special thanks to them for their inspiration, help and encouragement: and especially to 'Chief' Eric Ngalle Charles, Des Mannay, Xavier Panades I Blas, Manjit Sahota and Ian Thomas. Live Poets were also delighted to perform at the 2019 Marxism festival in London, and also at other events including the Merthyr Rising Festival and the Swansea Fringe.

During the pandemic, the international reach has been amazing once so many of us across the world discovered Zoom. This includes Poetry in the Brew from Nashville, USA, hosted by Christine Hall and Jo Collins, and Like a Blot from the Blue in Aberdeen, Scotland hosted by Fin Hall. We met many fine poets and I would especially like to mention Special K, Cathy Carson, Skylar, Michael Sindler, Bryan Franco, Markey Mark Symmonds, Mervyn DeepCobra Seivwright, Dane Ince, Tish Camp, Margaret O'Regan, Gary Huskisson, Catrice Greer, Michael Wilson, Erin Gannon, Pankhuri Sinha, Lesley Constable, Henry L. Jones, Noah Levin, Clive Oseman, Nick Lovell, Rick Spisak and Ian Preznansky. And every Monday night for the last year, our fellow-poet and musician Dave Clinch has hosted the Reform Inn open-mic sessions online from Barnstaple in Devon, where several talented musicians have treated us to some tremendous music.

I want to end by saying this. The secret ingredient in Live Poets – the element that, in my opinion makes it 'live' - is the fact that we are an organic part of Swansea's political and campaigning left. Many of us are activists as well as poets, involved in anti-deportation campaigns, anti-fascist work, support for the Palestinian struggle and the fight to protect the environment. We read poetry on demonstrations, rallies, vigils and picket lines. Our work doesn't exist in a vacuum: we aim to create a radical political culture through which people can understand the world in which they live, and through which, like the revolutionary students of 1968, they can show their realism by demanding the impossible.

In a world of war, plague and famine, the need for revolutionary change has never been greater. To again quote Trotsky: "Art might not be able to make the revolution but like a swallow it can herald the oncoming of Spring".

With our poetry let us show that another world is possible.

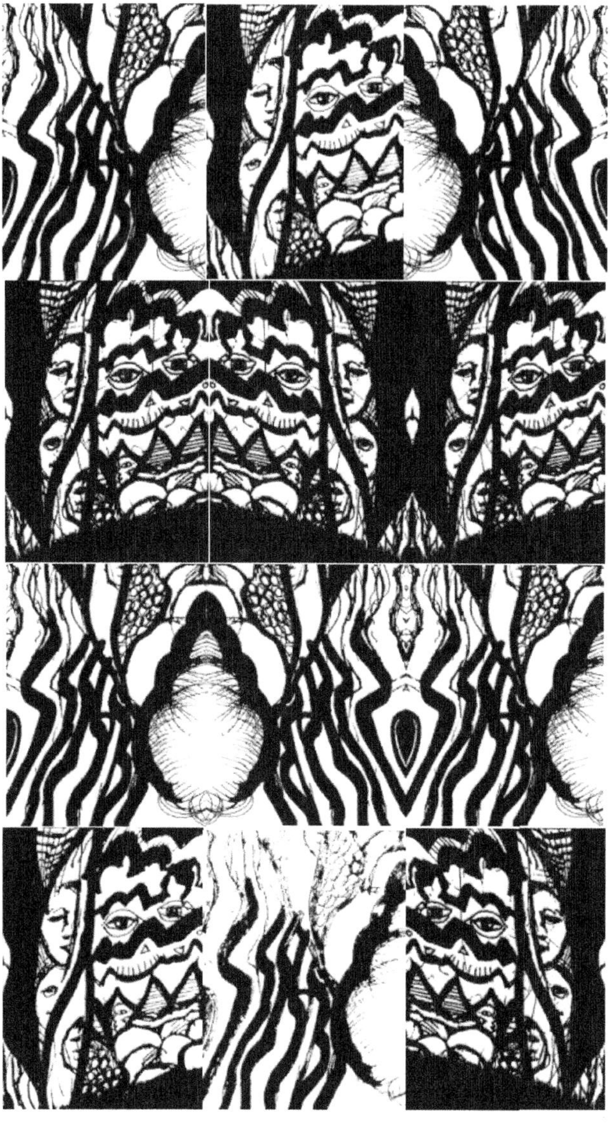

Reviews

Tim's work is brutally honest. It will open your eyes, for truly our society is crying out for change.
Eric Ngalle Charles - poet and playwright. Author of *I, Eric Ngalle*

Steel-strung, sexy storytelling with the silver-blue tinge of remembered, hot summer nights… these songs of love and revolution read like technicolour road movies… a joyous, turbulent ride through the upheavals of the 1960s, the Covid catastrophe, Grenfell, Vietnam, Iraq and the loves lost and won in human hearts. **Nicola Field – writer and activist, author of *Over the Rainbow***

All human experience is here. From the music of the 1960s, Janis Joplin, San Francisco, childhood, family, death, seaside towns, cats, love and politics to living in a plague world, there are no words here that do not connect with mind, body and spirit…
Carol Grimes – singer, poet and writer, author of *The Singer's Tale*

From love and sex to Janis Joplin and Boris Johnson's jaw dropping upper-class confidence in the face of his own incompetence, the themes of the poems in this wonderful new collection are richly diverse. They have in common great warmth, and a dedication to finding and telling truths, whether political, emotional, or pertaining to our flawed, chaotic, beautiful shared humanity.
Louise Raw, writer and activist, author of *Striking a Light*

'Bones of the Apocalypse is a call to action: a call to embrace our full humanity; to fight for justice and dance for joy (in equal measure); to stand together in solidarity. The blood of resilience pumps through the veins of every page, and it will leave you feeling ready for anything life might cast at your feet and throw in your face. We will triumph, even when living in the dust of the apocalypse'.
Jo Collins, government lawyer, moonlighting poet, and moderator at Nashville's *Poetry in the Brew*

Intoxicating and beautifully written poems. This collection reads like a play, each poem a glimpse of Tim's politics, history and passion. This is poetic dynamite so let the rulers shake in their boots!
Manjit Sahota, poet and Co-founder of Poets Against Racism

If books were weapons, this would be a well-aimed Molotov cocktail. 'If I were to meet you', has a whiff of 1968 about it, with its slogan from the student revolt in France – 'below the cobblestones, the beach...' Like Dave Widgery and others who lived through these times, Tim makes the point, 'we made music, but we didn't make the revolution'. But these poems are not just reminiscences, they are poetic reminders that the beach is still there, waiting to be exhumed from beneath the cobblestones...
Des Mannay, hooligan poet and performer, and author of 'Sod 'Em - And Tomorrow'.

Right from the start, these poems draw you in. Each poem tells its own story- the words painting vivid and detailed pictures, while simultaneously tying itself into the whole of the book. I was captivated by the depths of which each piece took me into life and memories of the author. This is a collection that soothes the soul and takes you on a trip down Memory Lane and back again. It is the kind of poetry collection you'll find yourself curling up in your comfy spot to read again and again.
Special K, spoken word artist and entertainer

Your poems have allowed me to travel across the globe and across different times. You show every side of yourself, the artist, the activist, the musician, the deep thinker, the lover. Thank you for sharing your talent with me and indeed my hope is yours, 'It surely can't be far to Revolution Time'.
Kemba Hadaway, trade union activist

'Bones of the Apocalypse' strikes your heart with needles of reality, and suffuses your soul with consciousness. You cannot escape the truth: you are living in a broken world in an uncertain future.
Xavier Panades I Blas, poet and activist, author of *Eternal Poet*

Tim's words are crafted with insight and understanding. "Who Killed Grenfell?" will leave you shaken. "Ode to the Tenby" is full of tantalising nostalgia. "Car Park" describes a snatched sensual moment - "they come together and for the briefest time are lost in the swell of the ocean".
Margaret O'Regan, poet and activist, Cork, Ireland

Other titles by Frequency House

Enter The Ziggurat (2021) by Gwion Iqbal Malik is the first publication by Frequency House. Iqbal is the Poet In Residence at the Dylan Thomas Birthplace in Swansea and Editor at Frequency House. His first publication 'Titans (Balboa Press) was released in 2015. *Enter The Ziggurat* is available to buy on Amazon and Frequency House.

The Frequency House Swansea Poetry Slam Anthology is the second publication by Frequency House. *The Anthology* is a look back at previous winners of the Slam as well as a selection of poets who have performed. *The Anthology* is a celebration of spoken-word poetry in Wales and the unique place it holds within the pantheon of poetry.

Printed in Great Britain
by Amazon